CW01432703

THE LEGEND OF FOLKLORE

THE LEGEND OF FOLKLORE

Terry A. Parker

&

Johnny G. Douglas

www.amazon.com/author/terryparker

Copyright © 2015 by Terry A. Parker

All rights reserved. No part of this publication may be reproduced or transmitted in any form or by any means, electronic or mechanical, including photocopy, recording, or any information storage and retrieval system, without permission from the copyright owner.

Printed in the United States of America

For my brother Jerry. You were my hero and I will always miss you.

This novel takes place five years after the happenings of
'The Kingdom of Folklore'.

PART I
The Garden

Chapter 1
Graham Berry, the Garden
&
The Stranger

The garden was large; almost filling up one entire side of the kingdom. It was here that Graham Berry was hard at work shoveling dirt to and fro. Many holes had been made here as if tiny-like graves. Some had been covered already; tiny mushrooms peeping their dome heads forth from the soil.

These would eventually turn into Smalls that would inhabit the kingdom. As all Smalls have in the past, these too would flourish, making Folklore thrive again.

Next to one particular hole lay a crude- crafted gardening tool. It resembled a rake in one aspect but a hoe in another. The apparatus was rather short, making the question up if it could have actually made the deep holes.

Like dried tree limbs, a miniature, rough-looking hand reached down, seizing up the tool. As it done so, a soft, blue silk-like sleeve collapsed downwards almost covering it completely up. On upwards, was Graham Berry, a tiny creature no larger than a pine cone.

He was old looking; ancient beyond his times. A blue robe fell to his tree-stump-looking feet making them vanish as if they were not there at all. Standing next to the holes, the old creature glanced around.

The Wiser's white beard dangled about the cool breeze, as his jagged ears folded backwards. Covering Graham's eyes were tiny, half-moon spectacles, where his red dimples grew as he grinned. Yes, he did indeed love this place; his garden.

Here, he would work for hours, hoeing this and that; making the dirt more fertile for the new Smalls to come. The garden gave Graham peace of mind; it was a place to escape to; a place to get away from it all. For the ancient Wiser, it was not a job but love that kept the garden of Mushers enduring.

Inspecting what he had done this very morning, he smiled once again; ears moving one at a time; back and forth as if fingers. This spot here was not finished as of yet, but the holes behind him were for he had finished it some days ago. Slowing turning around, he grinned yet again. There, almost an acre as well, were dozen-upon-dozen of mushrooms sprouting heavenward.

There were large ones, small ones, tiny ones and even some as large as tree trunks. They were of every color one could think of: blue, red, orange, pink and some multi-colored.

The Mushers appeared to vibrate with emotion and sound; the slightest wind, or a falling leaf would make them dance about, as the high sun shined across their tops making them glisten as if alive with joy.

And, why not? They were alive and soon would transform into living Smalls. In addition, these would live and thrive within the walls of Folklore, the Kingdom.

Graham Berry brought his ancient hand downward, caressing one particular mushroom's surface. It felt soft, pulsating with life.

The old one smiled, his dimples popped outwards, glowing a soft reddish color. Holding the gardening tool next to one side, the creature's eyes moistened with tears.

"Yes", he began in an ancient voice, "Pilgrim, my old friend, soon we will have more Smalls…more babies."

The golden mushroom did not respond, but the old one who had talked knew that it had felt his presence.

Graham Berry had buried Pilgrim under the soil many Dragonfly Overs Ago. The old Wiser knew it to be the right thing to do. If the tables had been turned, he was sure Pilgrim would had done the same for him.

Still stroking the mushroom's surface, the Wiser remembered back those many Dragonfly Overs Ago. In human terms, the Wiser knew it to be perhaps five years or more.

The fox had returned as foretold in Ka-Knear's Book of Laws. In its pages were written of a re-born fox and four baby Smalls that would return saving the Kingdom from the evil Ratz.

Beelzebub was the Ratz malevolent leader than. The creature had lost his paws in a battle with the Catz years before. In addition, he, Graham Berry, had battled with the demon-rat. It was even rumored that the Wiser had been killed at that time of warfare.

Replaced with razors and other attachments of war, the evil creature took over Folklore, imprisoning all of the Smalls beneath the ground within the Great Hall of Ka-Knear.

As Red Damion Foxx and the four Smalls lay seize to the kingdom's walls, Beelzebub used every trick and ploy at his disposal to slay them. Folklore itself could actually control and manipulate nature by the very magic that kept it going. The vines and elements that formed the kingdom also controlled the very nature that humans held dear.

If not for the kingdom being whole and complete, nature would run demoniacal, destroying everything on Mother Earth. Of course, earthquakes and storms were apart of how the world operated. Nevertheless, it was Folklore that kept it at bay.

Moreover, in the hands of the Ratz, the Smalls and humankind were at the mercy of all-out evil.

Side saddling the backs of felines, the fox with the four Smalls quickly advanced upon the kingdom with rock music feeling the air. It was this music that broke the sleeping spell of the catz.

Beelzebub's first trap of living vines and of a moving earth tsunami took them by surprise. Regrouping, they went for the massive walls of vines and thorns once again. Soon, they scaled them, entering the grounds of the kingdom.

Graham Berry could do little or nothing, as Beelzebub commanded his rat militias to assassinate Pilgrim, so a solitary arrow pierced his body as if the beginning of a morbid pincushion.

Not long after, the kingdom was finally saved; the evil ratz chased away and one of the Wisers' own locked away for aiding the Rat horde.

Returning his thoughts to the here-and-now, Graham Berry looked about the sprouting mushrooms with tears rolling down his cheeks. Yes, his friend, Pilgrim was gone (with Na-tuate now, as the Smalls referred to it) but his grave would remain…a new Musher soon emerging from it.

The old Wiser used the gardening tool to softly smooth out the soil beneath the proud mushroom. Doing this, he thought of Beelzebub and his top general, Black. They had fled the Kingdom on foot and onto the waterless highway. There, fighting amongst one another, an eighteen- wheeler ran them down.

The rat horde was a threat no longer.

The kingdom was rebuilt. Five years later, Graham Berry, Peer of the Realm, stood about his garden remembering the past. The truck drivers, Randy and Big Paul, had helped as well. They were the humans (Anti-Smalls, as they were referred to) that had unwillingly stumbled upon the kingdom of thorns and dead brush while out in the wild.

Unbeknown to the human, Randy, a Small had paid him a visit years earlier making him an Honorary Small. This fulfilled the prophecy in the

Book of Ka-Knear about an Anti-Small also being a savior to the kingdom.

Paul and Randy had a consultation with the large dragonfly called Jericho about where the Ratz would be. So, with this information, they were driving the truck that had ran down the two malicious Ratz.

The humans had not been heard from since and Graham figured they had went their separate ways as all humans had been known to do from time-to-time.

Slowing skimming the soil until it was to his liking, the Wiser stopped. Resting his head and hanging beard on the gardening tool's handle, he once again smiled; his ears pinned back with thought.

All-in-all, Folklore had been saved at that time. The Ratz were banished and their leader killed. For the last five years the kingdom had seen peace.

WC, the Wiser who had helped the Ratz with their evil plans, had been released from the Dwelling of Ta-Baa newest jail cell.

It was located near the highest hill of Folklore and surrounded by thick trees that allowed no sunlight to penetrate through. It was at this place, WC was placed after the ordeal of the Ratz came to an end. At least ten stories tall with a pathway of black rock leading to the front entrance, the once Wiser swore to take revenge against his fellow Smalls.

Graham Berry had the only key, and used it to release the Wiser.

WC was giving a choice to leave Folklore or
to remain and to be a good citizen. The Wiser took
the option of being a citizen without ever the chance
of becoming head of council within the court again.

Even though trusted again, the remaining
Wisers of Ka-Knear's Court let him free due to the
good of all Folklore.

WC accepted this as his fate, going about his
business as an ordinary Small with no chance of
ever becoming a Wiser within the Courts again.

Slowly turning, Graham Berry inspected the
empty holes once again. Soon, they would be filled
up giving birth to new Mushers. Afterwards, the
miniature Smalls would be taking to the nursery
where squirrels and other sorts of animals would be

their babysitters until they were big enough to live within the confines of the kingdom.

"Uncle! Uncle!" screamed a young voice from within the distant kingdom.

Glancing upwards, Graham saw his nephew running toward him. It was Dingle Berry who had been exiled years before, but only to return with the fox to save the kingdom. And save it, they did.

Behind Dingle Berry was the gigantic growth of vines and thorns forming the walls of Folklore. To an ordinary person it appeared as if just that: vines and brush, piled up in one mighty heap. It was circular in shape, giving the impression of a massive patch of stickers and thorns, nothing more.

The young Small jumped over some of the holes his uncle had dug as he dashed toward him.

Almost falling into one, he adjusted his run by leaping somewhat higher at times.

Dingle Berry had not changed much in the last five years. He had grown taller and bigger around the shoulders, but that was about it. The rest of him remained the same, resembling even more of a sock crammed with trembling jelly. This time, he was bare footed; his large feet and four toes visible. In his white outfit of a sleeveless shirt and grey trousers, he bounced toward his awaiting uncle.

"Slow down, Nephew!" replied Graham in a soft, firm tone. "You'll get here fast enough!"

He watched with a gleam in his eye as Dingle finally reached his side, bent over and out of breath.

"What is it that's so important?" the old Wiser questioned.

With his hands on his chubby knees, the young one caught a breath, slowly raising up. Even though five years older now he still was shorter than Graham.

"Uncle," he gleamed, "there's a stranger who wishes to speak with you!"

At the mentioning of a stranger, Graham Berry perked up. He quickly thought that maybe the person his nephew was replying about was Randy or Big Paul, the truck drivers. He quickly dismissed the thought as soon as it had occurred to him. Dingle Berry would had recognized the two Anti-Smalls who had helped with the saving of their home years earlier.

If not them, then who? This question plundered the old Wiser for a moment. Perhaps it was a forest resident requesting to speak with the ancient Small about some injustice done. Whoever it was, Graham dropped the wooden gardening tool.

"A stranger…you say?"

"Yes, Uncle. He says it's very important that he speaks with you right away?" The young Small was apprehensive, jumping up-and-down like a child right before his birthday, waiting to unwrap his presents.

"Than," began Graham Berry, "we mustn't keep this important stranger waiting any longer."

They turned, heading back toward the kingdom.

Behind them, the Mushers that had been sprouting out from their fresh dirt began to shake and vibrate like crazy. The spot where Graham had stood earlier (where the Wiser had buried Pilgrim) shook back and forth as if to pull itself free from the soil.

The stranger stood waiting at the entrance to Folklore. It was a three and a half foot tall weasel dressed up in a two-piece, black suit and tie that appeared just pressed to top notch condition. A silver, tiny metal briefcase dangled from his left hand.

If not for the fact this this was a weasel (walking upright as all animals did this close to the kingdom's magic) he might had been mistaken for a very, tiny business man.

The standing creature checked his right wrist now and again as if he were checking to see what time it was getting to be. However, the weasel wore no such attachments.

The front of Folklore slowly opened with sounds of crackling and snapping wood. The weasel stared in amazement as this unfolded. It appeared that someone had pulled back a stage curtain, revealing the interior of the kingdom.

Out of this entranceway stepped Graham Berry. He was by himself, walking slowly up to the awaiting weasel. The stranger to the kingdom greeted the Wiser with a firm handshake; something he had learned from the humans years ago.

"Hello, replied the weasel with a somewhat, halfway grin. His face appeared old and winkled, with black hair covering it with a touch of gray here and there. The eyes were very close together, making the creature seem as if he were up to no good.

Moreover, as far as Graham was concern, the weasel may very well be doing just that. The first impression the Wiser got was that the creature was dark with wickedness about his person.

The Wiser's eyes scanned the briefcase the stranger held at his side. It was metallic and square shaped and had what appeared to be some form of lock mechanism on the front of it.

"Yes," replied Graham Berry, "I've heard that you wanted to speak with me."

As if on cue, Dingle Berry eased up behind his uncle. His head popped out from side-to-side, as he too inspected the stranger. He was not showing his entire person; just hiding behind his ancient uncle playing peekaboo with his jelly-like cheeks shaking about.

As if looking for a timepiece, the weasel once again checked his wrist as if late for an engagement.

"Yes," he answered with almost an Irish accent. "I came as quickly as I could." He was watching Dingle Berry's head popping out from behind Graham's back: first, the left side than the right side.

"Is there a problem in which you seek council?" questioned Graham. Somehow he had the feeling that was not the case at all.

Feeling his nephew behind him, the ancient Wiser quickly turned, catching Dingle's head as it was just about to peep out to one side again.

The weasel watched this with weird curiosity. He had never seen such, at least not this close to the kingdom.

Dingle Berry quickly stopped in his tracks, knowing he was caught.

"Nephew," stated the Wiser, "what are ye doin'? We…" he glanced in the weasel's direction, than back to his nephew, "have…a guest here…and you act like you never seen one before."

"I just thought…" begin the Small, as Graham's fingers quickly cuffed his mouth from speaking.

"Now…Nephew…turn around and go back home…there is nothin' more to see here."

As if he had lost a war, Dingle Berry slumped his shoulders and slowly walked back to Folklore, his foot kicking a tiny peddle out of his path.

Watching him leave, Graham grinned, his old ears flapping to-and-fro. Turning back toward the stranger, he replied, "You must forgive my nephew…he's just curious is all."

The weasel seemed anxious.

"There's no need to apologize," he answered. "I understand fully. Now…I must have conference with you, Graham."

The old Wiser smiled, adjusted his spectacles, and than said, "For whom am I talking to, my dear friend?"

The walking animal in the two-piece suit looked into Graham's eyes, and slowly said, "I am…Salem. I've traveled a long way to get here."

He lifted the metal briefcase up, patting it. "In this matter I speak of…lies within this."

Graham's old eyes scanned the case, its lock and than to the weasel again. "Then…welcome, Salem. If it's talk you wish…than we shall continue inside."

The old Wiser motioned with an extended, stick-like arm towards Folklore's entrance. The weasel bowed, than walked into the kingdom. Graham followed, his ancient eyes taking in the metal briefcase once again.

Once inside the kingdom's grounds, the entranceway slowly shut leaving only a wall of vines, brush and thorns.

Within the courtyard the two walked side-by-side passing mud huts and other places of living quarters that stood on both sides of the street. Smalls were walking the avenues; some eyeballing

the stranger, while others appeared not to even
notice.

Passing one particular place, Salem (the weasel)
noticed that it had a sign out front that read 'Dr.
Acorn's Shop'.

Stopping out front, the two looked at the small
place. It was fashioned from massive leaves and
twisted vines creating a neat little shop that covered
a portion of the street that they walked.

"Dr. Acorn," Salem amused with a grin, while
pointing with a clawed hand. "My Uncle once
visited here. A great doctor indeed."

Graham glanced at the weasel as they continued
onward. From one of the store's window, Dr. Acorn
was filling acorn-like cups with sum sort of drink
resembling nectar. The doctor was short and fat,

wearing a white lab coat. Giant, round spectacles almost covered his entire face with a bushy mustache dangling below.

A little further up the trail, Graham and Salem came upon the Wiser's house that was a wide mud-hut with vines and mud coated its outside. Two, curved out windows were on either side of it giving the appearance that the home was very cool, or very hot depending on the weather.

"My home…Salem."

The Wiser gestured toward the place.

Salem grinned, scanning the place. "Yes, indeed a good home."

It appeared the mud-house had not been cleaned in years with books, plates and eating paraphernalia scattering the dirt floor like some weird, shaped carpet. Even the open windows had books piled up like strange, upside down curtains.

Walking inside the place, Graham grabbed up a twisted walking cane to push books from a toad-stool chair and something resembling a love seat.

"Excuse my place," the Wiser replied. "It appears my nephew hasn't got around to cleaning it up as of yet."

The weasel gleamed, looking at Graham. "No messier than mine…I assure you."

Taking a seat upon the chair, the Wiser watched as the stranger took the love seat. Feeling weird, Graham watched as the weasel put the briefcase on top of a wooden table separating the two seats.

Salem easily pressed three buttons on the lock and it suddenly snapped open. Lifting the metal case's led, the weasel eyed the Wiser, than slowly removed what appeared to be a very antediluvian envelope.

Graham looked at it with ancient eyes; his spectacles fell to the tip of his nose. Pushing them back up for a better fit, he grinned. Never had he witnessed anything as old as the envelope. Even the Book of Ka-Knear, old as it was, did not compare to what he beheld.

Noticing the stare of the Wiser, Salem undid the envelope and slowly pulled out an even older white piece of folded writing paper. Laying the envelope to one side, the weasel unfolded the paper in his rough claws and held it in front of him.

Graham had an eerie feeling creep over him. It was like, as the Anti-Smalls would say, his grave had been walked over. Slowly looking out the window, he saw his nephew, Dingle Berry who was next to Curly Sue, standing beneath a large, leafy bush.

He pretended not to see them; turning his old eyes back toward the weasel, Salem.

Salem had noticed the Wiser's stare as it looked about the outside and toward him again.

Graham Berry was not stupid; not by a long shot.

"I know that you are not here for council, Salem. What is it…exactly that you want with me?"

The weasel grinned. "Never said I was, Graham. Only that I had to speak with you."

The Wiser did not like the weasel's remark. He wanted to tell the creature to gather up the papers and leave. However…he was one of the Wiser's of Folklore. He could not go about saying, or even thinking such things. Besides, in a few short years he would be old enough to be an Elder. The only other Elder in the entire kingdom, since Pilgrim had been killed by the Ratz five years before.

He clasped his old, wrinkled fingers beneath his bearded chin, leaning forward. With a grin of his own, he replied, "So…Salem…I've noticed. Now…what are you here for…and why is this paper so important?"

The weasel smiled, revealing pointed teeth. Laying the paper on top of the table, he answered,

"You are right in one aspect…I am here for council."

Graham appeared stunned and confused.

"But…not mine, Graham: Yours! I'm here to give Folklore back…to its rightful owners!"

"What?" questioned Graham in somewhat anger. "What…do you mean, weasel?" His dimples turned blood red as his old fingers popped knuckles beneath his beard.

The weasel used two clawed fingers to spin the paper around so the Wiser could clearly see it. Even though old with age, the black-elf ink was clearly visible.

Picking it up, Graham leaned back into his chair. Bringing the writing paper in for a closer view, he read:

"Ka-Knear…my old friend…as you know as of five dragonfly overs ago…you lost the game of Kknear. The game you know was named after…I should say…for you."

Graham looked from the paper, to the weasel. The creature was leaning back in the love seat, twiddling his pointed thumbs. Ever now and then, Salem would check his right wrist as if checking the time as the humans did. However…he wore no watch; at least none the Wiser could make out.

Salem's squinted eyes stared at the Wiser as if staring right through him. Graham was not for sure, but he was sure as to what he was reading.

It was an ancient letter addressed to Ka-Knear himself. No documents in the kingdom came even close. Yes, some books here where written by the old one, but no documents written to him.

Graham's eyes once again fell onto the paper. The Wiser knew of the game called 'Kknear' and why Ka-Knear was named for it.

The Wiser recalled an ancient myth of his predecessor. It stated that on the very night of Ka-Knear's birth, his parents were playing the game.

It was a game that very few still played today. That was because it was basically 'winner-take-all'. The night Ka-Knear sprung from a musher, his father (Bas-Knear) was very deep into the game.

The game consisted of four pinecones of different colors: usually red, blue, black and orange. Red was for the eyes of the Earth's sun as it rose and sat; blue was for the oceans, streams and waters that made life possible; black was for the night; and last, but not least, orange was for danger of life (like the orange mushrooms that were stationed just outside the Forbidden Zone).

The play itself was simple, but the outcome never was. One placed the four pinecones into a wooden basket that was shaken up afterwards. Then the basket was quickly placed upside down, not knowing where the cones fell, or where the colors lay. At that moment…everything was random.

One would bet on something – say, their home, food, magic twigs, and other assortment of items. In one particular case, Graham recalled, a Small had gambled, losing his mate playing the game of Knear.

The object of the game was to say what color you wanted: red, blue or black. The orange cone was always the loser; sort of like snake eyes were the Anti-Smalls in the game of dice.

If a Small said 'blue' and reached under the basket and got the blue one, he would then make a wager. Then, the cones were reshuffled and placed beneath the basket once again. However, if he failed to do so, he had to try again for the blue cone. If he would fail a second time, then he made a wager regardless.

To win, the Small would have to recover the blue cone. If successful, the other one playing would lose whatever was wagered on.

If a Small said 'blue' and retrieved the orange one, he lost automatically everything he owned – wager and all. Everything: the Small's home, magic twigs, any mushers you may had been growing at the moment…and yes, even his mate.

The game had been banned from the kingdom as far back as Graham could remember. In addition, if memory served him well, the ancient Wiser knew that the last Small to play it was Bas-Knear.

Nevertheless, if the letter was genuine, than it was not Bas-Knear who had played it last, but Ka-Knear himself.

The old Wiser wondered why the founder of Folklore would even try to play such a game of chance…and a banned one at that?

What Bas-Knear lost was not really nothing major: Just an ancient tablet that contained nothing important. After that, Ka-Knear was born from a musher and named Ka-Knear…after the game itself.

Returning his old eyes to the next sentence of the letter, Graham Berry read on:

"Since you got the orange cone…you have lost all that is yours: The kingdom for one. You may keep everything else, since you have lost so much already."

The Wiser could not believe what his eyes beheld. Ka-Knear gambled away Folklore? It couldn't have happened? The weasel was wrong…or lying threw his jagged teeth!

Not able to remove his old eyes from the paper, he continued reading:

"And…Ka-Knear…my friend…as for you being an honest and dear friend…you and the Smalls can remain at Folklore for 2000 dragonfly overs. At 2001, the kingdom retrogresses to me…and mine."

It was signed on the very bottom, far right corner:

"Your friend… Jeremy Bentham Rat".

After finishing the ancient letter, Graham went ballistic. He quickly stood up, threw the paper toward the weasel's face, and grabbed up his nearby magical twig. Pointing it directly at Salem, the Wiser slammed:

"This is nonsense, Salem, you are a fraud and liar! You…are in cahoots with the Ratz themselves!! Leave Folklore at once…or I'll have you thrown out…do you hear!"

The weasel did not seem afraid by the Wiser's remarks, or for that matter that a magic twig was aimed his way. He easily collected the letter, folded it neatly, and returned it back inside the envelope, than stood.

"Think what you will, Graham, but it's all true and can be proving!"

"Out!" the Wiser spat one last time, his old hand shaking, holding the twig.

"For now," replied the weasel. "But I will return with the magistrate…Bob Beaver." He saw the look in Graham's eyes. It was almost a split second of pure disbelief, than terror, than it was gone.

"Yes, you do know him, Graham. Moreover…in a few days I shall return with him. I tried the easy way out: talking. However, that got us nowhere fast, as I thought would happen. So…I've no choice."

He replaced the envelope back inside the metal briefcase and closed it. And with a flip of a pointed claw, he re-locked it.

Graham just stood there, still aiming the magic twig.

"Oh, and yes, he will hear about how you treated me. It won't look good for you at all, my friend. The magistrate doesn't go easy with this sort of treatment!"

Turning, Salem walked out of Graham's door and down the straw- covered street.

As he left, Graham collapsed into his mushroom chair; the magic twig fell from his hand, striking an open book, and went still.

It can't be, the old Wiser thought with grave sorrow. His jagged ears were pinned all the way back, almost to his wrinkled neck. How…could it be? After all of the wars Folklore has had…and lived through…that the Ratz owned it…legally?

The thoughts burned itself deep inside Graham's mind like a poison he was giving that would not just kill him, but every last Small in the kingdom.

Under Folklore, in the Great Hall of Ka-Knear, a trial had been thrown together for better or worse. Not a trial as in unruly Smalls but to determine what was to transpire between the kingdom and Salem, the weasel.

It was some hours later after the stranger had left. Dingle Berry and Curly Sue had rushed into Graham's home after hearing him raising his voice to the weasel. Of course, the creature had just left as the two young ones stepped inside.

There, they beheld an unusual sight indeed. Sprawled about his mushroom chair like someone who had just lost everything in the world, Graham appeared sick. Not physically sick but like a person with all the problems of the world on their shoulders.

His hands were dangling on either side; his magic twig lay nearby on the dirt floor, resting in an open book.

Curly Sue approached first, followed by Dingle Berry, as they both slowly walked over to the Wiser's side. He did not seem to notice them at first, than seconds later, stared at them. A small tear ran from underneath his spectacles and onto his rosy cheek.

"Uncle," quietly asked Dingle, "what is wrong?"

Curly Sue had her small hands behind her back.

"Was it the…stranger?" she questioned with a soft tone.

The girl had not changed much in the five years since they had won back the kingdom. She still looked like a smart college girl with longer blond hair now hanging way passed her backside. Curly Sue had long lost the ponytail style of years past. The round, framed glasses still covered her doll-like face with pointed, soft-pink ears wriggling from either side of her hair.

"On…it's nothin'" Graham halfway replied. "Nothin' like that…I assure you."

The Wiser slowly looked to where his magic twig had fallen. The old, elf made wand had crisscrossed pages of an ancient book so happened to be called 'Ka-Knear's Journal of Games'. Picking up the elm-made twig, Graham easily stood up, with the two younger Smalls beside him.

The girl could not remember a time when Graham was like this; not in the six years that she had grown to know and love him. She could not help but wonder what had went on between the Wiser and the weasel. It had to have been awful... just awful.

Graham looked about his home: the thrown about books, pots and pans and dishes everywhere. For the first time, in a very long time, he felt as if he was looking at it for the last time.

Coming back to his senses, he replied, "Out ya go. Go out and play…or whatever it is you kids do nowadays."

They both stared at him with curiosity; than turned and slowly left the house.

Graham easily walked from his home and onto the straw-covered street. Glancing about Folklore, the Wiser saw Smalls and other assortment of forest animals walking about.

Funny, he amused to himself, as he slowly advanced down the street, that maybe real soon they wouldn't have a place to call home. It all seemed so surreal to him: the meeting with Salem, the weasel, and of the ancient note stating the Ka-Knear had lost Folklore to the very evil they had fought against numerous times in the past: the Ratz!

Below Folklore within the Great Hall of Ka-Knear, Graham was seated upon a tall, mushroom type stool. Next to him sat U.B. Einstein, Elvis and DM, the General Patton lookalike. WC was not a Wiser any longer, but resided within the courtroom nonetheless.

WC sat at some circular tables up front with almost all of the kingdom present. Even Sprouting

News had taking up almost one entire corner of the place; their writing parchments ready for action. It would appear that something very big was about to take place. Never had the Wisers ordered everyone to the hall at such short notice.

Chairs were seated about the entire courtroom with almost no room to walk as mummers echoed throughout the underground room.

"I heard rumors that that stranger that met up with Graham was someone very high up in the courts," replied an old looking Small with a walking cane shaped like a snake laying across his lap.

"No," stammered another old Small with gray hair and missing an ear, "I 'eard he was wanting a hearing of some sort!"

The rumors quickly spread across all of the Smalls as if ocean waves of whispers. Even WC seemed at odds to what was going on. Never had Folklore ever requested everyone to be present in the Great Hall…and never without posting the meeting days before.

The mummers grew louder still as U.B. Einstein grabbed up his owl-shaped gravel, striking the table in front of him three times. Each hit was louder than the first, until he almost broke it on the third try.

"Order! Order!" he yelled so all could hear.

As quick as the mummers started, they stopped.

Graham Berry slowly stood up from his chair and addressed the assemblage.

"People…of the kingdom…I know you wonder why you have been summoned here…and on very short notice."

Smalls in the hall all had their eyes upon the old Wiser and Peer of the Realm. Dr. Acorn was seated out in front, a book held tightly in his right hand entitled 'U Can Lose 3 Acorn Sizes Too!'.

The middle-age Small was chubby with a blond beard dangling from his pointed chin. Large, over-sized, round glasses covered his eyes with his bent, pointed ears holding them in place.

Next to the Dr. was seated Curly Sue and Dingle Berry, dressed in long, flowing blue garments.

WC twisted somewhat, eyeing Graham with contempt and wonder.

"First of all," begin the Peer of the Realm, "I want each and every one of you here to know what I am about to say could be completely false."

At this, mummers started once again than quickly stopped.

"Today, my dear Smalls, a visitor came to me…with news of our kingdom; news of grave concern!"

The Sprouting News reporters quickly took notes; their ink-filled quell pens were going overtime on the writing parchments.

WC quickly stood, pointing a crooked finger at the Wiser. "What is this… Graham…what is this all about? First…we're told to gather here…" he gestured with a hand about the seating area, indicating all of the citizens within.

Graham stared at WC who stood like a sore thumb among the mists of Folklore's inhabitants. He knew WC was not really concerned about what he had to say, or for anyone else for that matter. The ex-Wiser only wanted to deface the high court; to make them all pay the way he had to in the Dwelling of Ta-Baa, the kingdom's prison.

"WC…I assure you…if you just listen, you will hear!"

The ex-Wiser did not stop there, still pointing an incriminating finger at Graham. "Yes," he spat, "let's hear what you have to say!" With that, he slowly sat back down, arms crossed over his chest.

Graham knew that this was not a good thing. With the news he had, he was sure WC would mode it and shape it until it fitted him perfectly.

"Like…I said…it could all be false; a pack of lies."

The Wiser watched as the Smalls within shuffled about in their mushroom-type chairs; Dr. Acorn easily sipped from a wooden cup in front of him; and WC just eyed all of the Wisers, one at a time.

Graham went on: "The stranger, Salem, showed me documents…stating that Folklore…" his old eyes shifted to and fro, from one Small to the next, "was…lost …to…"   For the first time in a very long time, the Wiser's was at a lost for words.

How could he actually say what he had to say? What would transpire next? Moreover…how would WC use this for his advantage?

As if on cue, U.B. Einstein slowly stood up next to Graham, dabbing his old friend's shoulder, letting him sat back down.

"What…Graham is trying to say…is that this particular stranger… Salem… has papers stating that Folklore belongs…to the…Ratz!"

Outrage ran among the Smalls like a fever. Some screamed, while others stared in all-out terror. The news reporters dropped their writing pens, and even Dr. Acorn's book fell from his reach.

WC leaped back up with grave anger in his eyes.

"The ratz?" he yelled in shock. "How in Ka-Knear's name is this possible, U.B.?"

U.B.'s hands were placed firmly on the table in front of him as he slowly looked to his comrades, than WC again.

A word could not be said at that moment as the Smalls' voices grew louder than before.

"Quiet!" he yelled to no prevail.

Grabbing the gravel, U.B. hit it on the table several times, but it did no good. The voices grew steadily louder like someone turning the volume up on a radio.

WC grabbed up his wooden drinking vessel and threw it toward the fireflies above them. The wooden cup flew upwards, scattering the insects there creating a temporary darkness that easily faded with light prevailing again. The drinking vessel struck the ceiling with a clang then to the floor where it laid motionless.

The temporary darkness had worked. The Smalls in the courtroom quieted down, then went silent.

U.B. looked at WC; his eyes squinted with grave anger.

"How in Ka-Knear's name...you ask, WC? According to Salem...it was Ka-Knear himself that lost our kingdom and Salem is going after the magistrate, Bob the Beaver, as we speak! If that happens..."

The Smalls remained quiet this time around; across their faces were fear beyond fear.

Even WC went into total quiet.

U.B. slowly reached for his blue, elf-made smoking pipe that was shaped like that of a seahorse. Passing it from hand-to-hand, he easily lit it with a flick of a bent twig. A miniature flame left the tip of the wand, quickly sparking the crumbled leaves below.

With the pipe between his ancient lips, he inhaled, happily as the sensation of lambus weed entered his lungs. Almost at once, he felt relaxed.

U.B. thought of the lambus root that grew beyond the mushers of Folklore, deep within the forest. Funny, as he recalled the weed.

It grew deep in the forest; past the swamps and streams, next to a line of tress and next to the trail of no return as the Smalls called it. This road led to a valley.

The valley was dark and deep as he remembered it. Something else about the place ate at his brain as his ears flipped to and fro. What was it? The thought burned itself into his head as it slowly came to him. There, alone and isolated, was the Kingdom Tree.

It sat on the valley floor with no other trees for miles around. It had no leaves; its limbs resembled skeleton arms stretching outwards. It was here, long ago, that U.B. recalled visited it with his father.

The Folklore Tree could be their only hope for a future. With its wisdom of millions of dragonfly overs, it could possibly be the Smalls only hope.

"What are you doing?" questioned Graham, noticing his peer as he just stared into empty space.

"Yes," said WC in a calmer voice, as he watched the Wiser blowing smoke from his sea horse shaped pipe. The blue smoke climbed upwards towards the ceiling where it rested with the fluttering dragonflies.

U.B. slowly came back to the here and now.

"I may know how to save us...and the kingdom."

"Well," retorted WC, "how is that going happen when that weasel is headed for Bob the Beaver?"

U.B. Einstein adjusted his spectacles and stared about the courtroom.

"We must...talk with the Folklore Tree!"

Everyone within the assembly seemed stunned at the statement. It has been eons since anyone has spoken to the tree...or asked it for help. And then, it was only written in stories and myths.

The remaining Wisers all stared at U.B. as he puffed from his pipe. They, too, could not believe what they had just heard.

Chapter 2
Grahams Abode, The Meeting

&

the Suitcase

The trial was in midway when most of the Smalls were escorted outside. U.B. had called for recess because of all the loudness that erupted right after the stillness. The news reporters appeared afraid to even print what they had just heard.

As the last remaining citizen left the hall, U.B. and the other Wisers went to a large, toadstool, shaped table. Setting upon chairs that encircled it, they all eyed one another.

Graham Berry scratched his long, white beard and adjusted his spectacles. This meeting, he realized, was going to be the most important one of all the ones in the past. It was to determine the outcome of their home: The Kingdom of Folklore.

The fireflies had settled down upon the ceiling letting the light simmer somewhat. The activity from the flying cup had long been forgot about.

Graham looked about his friends and than the surroundings. Could it really be possible that he could be viewing the hall for the final time? He prayed to Ka-Knear that it was not.

Than again...if the circumstances were true, than it was the founder himself that brought about Folklore's demise.

"What can we do?" questioned WC, as he was permitted to remain behind with the Wisers. After all, he was once one himself.

Einstein positioned himself better in his chair, rubbing his curly beard with a grin. It was not a grin of happiness, but rather a grin of friends helping friends.

"We must locate the Folklore Tree, my friends. From there we may be able to find the greatest of all Wisers." His ears flipped forward for a bit, than back to their normal position.

"Yes," replied Graham, "but than again...the tree is a myth...a legend, not to mention Bob. It has been read to our children as bedtime stories...and nothin' more. Even ourselves, as babies, have heard of the tales. They could be nothin' more than that."

Silence surrounded them as the words soaked in.

"Myths and legends," cried WC to all. "We are putting our trust in U.B. and Graham? How do we even know the kingdom has been compromised? What...if the weasel lied?"

WC's eyes scanned Graham for a second as he waited for an answer.

"We...don't, yet!" answered Graham. "For now...all I have is the weasel's words...and the ancient letter that I read."

Slowly standing, Graham wobbled toward the crystal wall that was used at the little ones' trial years ago. Removing a crystal from a shelf of similar ones, he tapped the wall seven times. At the final tap, the mighty wall flickered, coming alive with what transpired between Graham and the weasel earlier on.

The Wisers and WC watched as Salem revealed the briefcase and what it concealed. They witnessed

Graham reading the old letter and of what happened next as the Wiser ordered the weasel to get out.

"Therefore," begin Graham, "we must find the tree and ask if this is true...or a pack of lies."

Everyone within the assembly agreed upon what had to be done. Standing, they applauded the Wiser for his courage.

Later that evening, Graham invited his friends into his adobe. Within the small house, amongst the scattered books, sat WC, Graham Berry, and U.B. Einstein. The rest was asked to remain outside within their own houses. Here, the Wisers were planning on finding a way to discover the Folklore Tree.

It had been eons since anyone had even seen the tree, and then it was merely tales and myths. The last one to visit it was U.B. Einstein and that was with his father. And then, he was but a child and could had just imagined being there.

There were so many places and trees, Einstein's father could of said that it was the Folklore Tree. Who could know for sure but than again, they would have to try. Even if it was only myth, it was the Kingdom's only chance.

Around nine, U.B. was thumbing through an ancient book entitled, 'The Tree of the Kingdom'. Within its pages, written in black elf ink, was the description of what the tree looked like and where it may have been located.

Seated around a toadstool table were the main ones responsible for locating the tree.

WC, Einstein and Graham Berry were going through book after book trying to find out if the tree was real or not.

In a far off corner of the place a spider web started to vibrate as if insane. It was a message from a snail-mail that someone was sending.

Slowly standing Graham Berry approached the web. It was indeed some sort of mail that they were getting. The Wiser could not recall the last time mail was delivered to his house.

"Well...what does it say?" questioned WC with curiosity.

Touching the tiny threads of web, Graham easily read the message.

"It says, my friends, that Salem has not yet visited the magistrate…Bob Beaver. The weasel also says that maybe he was hasty…taking off the way he did, and that he is sorry."

The others in the house eyeballed Graham as he read the snail mail.

"He says that he will give us seven days…in human terms…to vacate the premises. After that…he will than pay Bob a visit if he has to."

U.B. Einstein slowly came up to his old friend's side, putting a hand on his shoulder.

"Than…my old friend…that gives us a week to locate Bob ourselves."

"But how…and where do we look?" questioned WC, advancing toward his friends as well.

Graham turned facing his comrades. In his eyes lay the answer.

"First...we must find the Folklore Tree. From there...we can discover if it is true about what Salem says...and then we can ask about the magistrate's whereabouts."

At that moment, the Wisers and once-Wiser clasped their hands together. What had to be done...had to be done.

Around eight at night, Curly Sue and Dingle Berry stood behind Graham's home. They had been eavesdropping for the past 20 minutes, hearing all that transpired within the place.

Slowly leaving the broke vine that made it easy for them to hear the voices within the house, the twosome walked up the street somewhat. Coming to a halt next to Curly Sue's place, they walked inside.

Her house was pink as pink could be. Even the straw-covered walls appeared pink, with pictures of her family hanging here and there.

Furniture sat neatly about the place with the cleanness of a girl. Her parents had moved across to the other side of the kingdom letting her have this place as was promised.

School had long been out for her, giving her more freedom to find a job within the kingdom. Sue had worked several weeks for Dr. Acorn, filling this cup with that and cleaning up the place or trying to sell anything new he may had stumbled across.

The work was not hard, but actually boring. But it made her parents very proud of their daughter.

"Love your place," Dingle Berry said, taking a pink toadstool for a chair with his large feet propping up on a love seat, his four toes wriggling like worms.

Taking a seat herself, Curly Sue grinned. "You always say that when you come in here. And...please remove your feet from that. You haven't washed them in weeks I'm sure."

Slowly removing his feet, Dingle Berry sat up in the chair with his grey trousers falling, covering his feet up.

"I just washed up the other night," he said softly, creasing his pants down more, hiding everything.

"Whatever, cuz," remarked Sue with thought. "We've got bigger fish to fry than your bathing habits. What did you make out of that we heard?"

She was still wearing her flowing blue garments she had on earlier.

"What Uncle Graham said?"

"What else?" Sue questioned, her eyes rolling in her head.

Dingle Berry grinned. "Oh...that! The Folklore Tree and all. Sounds surreal, huh? I think it's been sometime since anyone has even considered the tree."

Curly Sue rubbed her red, round spectacles with thought.

"You know...I've been to it before."

"No way...when?"

Playing with her long, blond hair that was sprawled about her back, she answered, "Professor Biggs class in Grade A...you remember."

Dingle scratched his dark hair for a moment, than replied, "Yeah...okay... I'll buy that, cuz. But I thought in that Collection Society, you just went 'round stealing from Anti-Smalls' homes and stuff."

Curly Sue grew furious. "We didn't steal, Dingle. We borrowed things to study. Let's get back to the point at hand...can we?"

"Sure...why not."

"Well...once while the Professor and I were...borrowing...things from a certain home...we found what looked like a Small's ID card."

At the mentioning of this, Dingle Berry's ears easily flowed all the way back to his neck line with wonder. "Really...was it an ID card...and how did it get there?"

"Well...we wanted to make sure so Mr. Biggs wanted to visit the Folklore Tree and ask it. That's one of the first times I ever heard a Small say that. All this time I thought it a myth."

The girl slowly got up, went to the kitchen and poured herself some blueberry juice. Making one for Dingle too, she gave it to him and sat back down.

"Than what?" wondered Dingle, leaning all the way forward and in danger of falling from the toadstool.

"Well, we went deeper into a part of the forest I've never been to before. Professor Biggs may me promise to never tell anyone 'bout where we were going or what we were about to see. I did."

Curly sipped the juice, than continued:

"Way past the Zoned Mushrooms we walked...collecting acorns, insects and holding what we thought was an ID card from the kingdom. It took 'bout five hours...but we finally entered this massive, empty valley. It appeared that it had been wiped out by a massive twister or somethin'."

Her hands circled the air several times trying to simulate what she was saying, as her blueberry juice splashed about her wooden cup.

Dingle Berry's eyes grew large with excitement as his cheeks rolled like trembling jelly. Never had he heard a tale such as this his cousin was telling.

"Than what, Sue? What happened then?"

Calming down, she grinned, put her glass down on a mushroom table in front of her.

"Then...Dingle...I saw it! Alone...and by itself...was

this ancient- looking tree with no life it appeared. Its leaves were all gone giving the looks of bony arms and hands.

"We slowly approached it...the Professor first...than I behind."

Dingle Berry closed his eyes shut trying to visualize what his cousin was saying. He had heard about the Folklore Tree as well from his parents. They were even going to try and find it before when he was charged and exiled from the kingdom. But, alas, they did not know where to search...or even began looking.

"At the tree, the Professor used one of the acorns he had found, easing it into a small notch on the tree's bark. It appeared to fit perfectly, than it was gone like that. It was like it became part of the tree.

"Than before I knew it...the tree jumped and started shaking like a mighty wind had just blown up."

"You mean it jumped out of the ground?"

"No, silly, it just...jumped. I can't explain it no more than that. But a few second later...it talked. I didn't know it at first, but the busted and cracked tree had lines and circles about its bark, 'bout midways up. This was what spoke. The lines weren't lines at all...but the tree's eyes, nose and mouth!"

Dingle just about fell from his seat as he heard the words. A talking tree!! No way, he thought.

Getting into a better position, he listened on as Sue went on:

"Well, to make a long story short, the tree asked what we wanted with it. It wasn't like you and I are talking, but rather like the wind. But...you could understand it and all. 'Why have you awaking me?' it asked. The voice was like one of the old Elders but older...like an old man who hasn't talked in years.

"Biggs showed the ID card to the tree...and one of its limbs just reached out and took it. Just like that, it did. Tiny, skeleton branches wrapped about the card, then it brought it right up to what I suppose was its eyes."

The girl grew quiet, finishing her juice. Dingle Berry almost went ballistic, wanting to know what transpired next.

"Don't stop there, cuz, what did the tree say?"

Looking across her cup's top, Curly eyes appeared to grow larger behind her round glasses. "Believe it or not, Dingle, it was an ID card from the kingdom. It belonged to our lawyer, Red Damion Foxx. He had somehow left it there...the tree didn't know how for sure.

"It said that maybe the fox had left in a hurry...as he was known to do while trying to steal chickens for supper."

"Oh," Dingle replied, "the place was some sort of farmhouse...with those birds 'n all living there."

"Yea," she replied, "it was a farmhouse alright. Seems the farmer there must had discovered the card, bringing it inside for a closer look."

A loud noise suddenly came from Curly Sue's bedroom. It sounded as though someone, or something, had broke through her glass window pane there.

Jumping with fright, the two looked at each other, than dashed for the room through a beaded doorway, Curly Sue first, with her cousin tailing behind. He didn't seem real interested in finding out, or seeing for that matter, what it was.

Once inside her bedroom, they quickly saw what resembled a large opossum jumping from the window seal and into the darkness beyond. Racing to the broken window pane, they both glanced outside. They saw nothing but pitch black with lights of nearby houses reverberating about the straw yard.

"What...what was it?" asked a terrified Dingle Berry, his body quivering more than ever.

"Don't know," Sue answered, backing up from the window with her cousin by her side.

It appeared nothing within the bedroom had been touched. The single, pink bed was still next to the far wall, looking as if it had just been made. The mushroom-type dresser sat next to the doorway with some of its doors half open.

As if on cue, Curly Sue inched to the dresser, pushed a few underclothes back inside and quickly closed it. That is when it caught her eye. In the other far corner of the room, under more pictures of her family, was a very small, square-shaped, blue suitcase.

It was laying upon the floor and appeared to be locked.

"What the..?" she questioned the air.

"What, cuz? What is it?" asked Dingle Berry, inching ever so slowly toward Sue. Halfway there, he saw it to.

"A...a...suitcase!" he exclaimed, as if he had never seen one before.

"Yes," said the girl Small, as she easily approached it.

"Be careful!" said Dingle Berry, who was still in shock over the thing that had tried to break in his cousin's house. But now, he had this to add to his worries. With a glance now-and-than towards the broken window, he prayed to Ka-Knear that whatever did the deed did not decide to come back.

Curly Sue inched toward the blue suitcase, being mindful of Berry's concern. Right next to the bag, she easily reached down for a closure look. A zipper wrapped around its front, so Sue gracefully unzipped it.

After it was done, the Small slowly and carefully opened the flap.

Within it was a piece of folded writing paper and what appeared to be some sort of compass.

"Be careful, Sue," repeated Dingle, right behind her left shoulder.

"Heard you the first time," Curly Sue said with a stern glance his way.

Taking the contents of the suitcase, she put them on top of her bed, laying them evenly out.

Looking at Dingle, she said, "Quick...close that curtain so no one can see!"

"That window?" he said, spying the broken window pane once again with a swallow of somewhat fear.

"Yeah...and hurry up!"

With apprehensiveness, he easily went up to the window. With a quick glance about the darkness outside, he saw nothing more than shadows and flickering lights. Grabbing the pink curtain, he lowered it down so the window was not visible from beyond.

He was at Sue's side by the bed in no time. There, neatly laid out, were the contents from the suitcase: a folded piece of paper and a black, round-shaped compass.

"What...what are they?" he questioned, easily looking from the contents to his cousin than to the contents again.

Curly Sue slowly sat upon the bed, and with a look of wonder, she slowly reached for the letter. Unfolding it, she noticed that something was written on it in what appeared to be blue, elf ink.

Holding up the letter, she started to read, as Dingle Berry sat next to her.

"Dear Friend Sue. It has been all too long since we have met or even talked. If you are reading this, you know that I have long since departed this world and have entered the Na-tuate world."

The girl looked up from the note and eyed her cousin with a smile of hope. With tears filling up her eyes, she easily wiped them away with a tiny finger. Curly Sue instantly knew who was responsible for the letter and compass. It was her Grade A teacher from the Collection Society of so many years ago, Professor Biggs.

Looking back to the letter, she continued as Dingle Berry watched in amazement.

"Dear Sue...do not mourn me for I am with what I loved the most: nature. And I'm sure this note has come to you at the most treasured time when you need me the most. My trusted consort, Frank Opossum, has been waiting til the exact moment when you may need help the most.

"I have told him many Dragonfly Overs ago to watch over you and take care of you and others about the kingdom. With him, I entrusted the compass that came with the letter you are reading."

Curly Sue wiped away more tears as memories of the professor engulfed her. She recalled many a time that they went into Anti-Smalls' houses searching for treasures that they could return with.

She heard of his passing sometime back and she had went into the forest for a cry. But, afterwards, she thought she would never hear from him again.

"I...don't believe it?" replied Berry with shock. "The Professor has had that opossum watching over you...and most likely me as well?"

"Well...yeah...he did care 'bout me deeply...and you too. Ever since we were exiled five years ago...he has been worried. He even told me one day that he would watch after us.

"Too bad Rusty and the baby aren't here to witness this with us."

"I know, cuz, but they had to leave...visiting a sick uncle or somethin' in the town of Simms. Didn't never have a chance to go there myself, but I heard there is a Small community there...made up to confuse the ratz if they ever came back here."

Curly Sue grinned, pushing her glasses up for a better fit.

"I know, Dingle. I miss 'em to, you know. Maybe soon we can visit them, ok."

Dingle smiled, shaking his head, as Curly Sue picked up the compass, studying it. It was round and black with the needle pointing North as all compasses did. Placing it back down onto the bed, Sue continued reading:

"The compass will help you search for what you are seeking, my dear girl. Just ask of it what you seek, and it shall tell you directions of getting there. Yes, I shall speak with you from the device as I have excogitated my voice from within its contents."

Her and Dingle Berry shared incredulities about what she had just read.

"No way, cuz?" was all Berry could muster at that moment, looking from the compass in Sue's hand to her once again.

Curly Sue wanted so much to ask the compass a question, but she knew that she had to finish the letter first if nothing else.

Glancing at the letter once more, she read on:

"In Frank shall visit you soon with more details. I know he most likely came to you in a weird sort of way...but as far now he must do so. He will explain more to you later about that and other things.

"Your friend forever, Professor Jerry D. Biggs."

With more tears, she removed her glasses and wiped them away. Slowly putting them back on, Curly Sue took the letter back to the suitcase, folded it, and put it inside. Zipping it back up, she close the flap noticing that it had a large letter 'B' embroidered on the case's outside.

"Now...what?" questioned Berry, as Sue joined him at the bed once more.

She smiled, picked up the compass and said, "Let's ask Professor Biggs!"

Chapter 3

Gathering, Searching & Looking About

The sun slowly revealed itself about the outside world as Graham Berry stood within his mushroom garden with curiosity. He could not believe his eyes as what they beheld. There, were Pilgrim's remains had been buried was empty. It would appear that the soil had been removed and something, or someone, had stepped from it.

Could it be, the old Wiser marveled, that Pilgrim was born once again? He quickly dismissed the thought even though he had wished it so. The musher must had been ready and simply pulled itself out to join the kingdom.

But if that be the case, he thought, than where was it? It had to be just a baby and needed attention from the nursery. He would check it out later, but for now he must recover the hole and plant another mushroom for birth.

Scratching his long beard, he pulled on his grey ears as if to pull them off. Never had he witnessed such a thing. He looked this way and that, but to no prevail. What on Ka-Knear's world was going on, he questioned to himself.

Looking toward the Kingdom, he saw Curly Sue and his nephew coming his way, so he quickly covered up the hole, finishing it with his foot as they came closer.

He did not want them to get the wrong impression or start a panic or the exact opposite. They might believe someone dug Pilgrim up!

As the two young ones approached him, he stood in front of the hole, hands behind his back.

"Uncle! Uncle!" cried Dingle, as they was right next to him now.

"What's the fuss, young ones?" Graham replied, all the time keeping a foot on top of the fresh dirt.

"Look what Sue found last night!"

So Curly explained to Graham about the encounter the night before, and of the note and compass.

Hearing this, Graham quickly grabbed each one by the hand and lead them inside of Folklore and into his house. Within the living room, Graham cleaned off his table by knocking every book and dish from it. They struck the floor, laying there.

"The compass, Sue, let me see it, please."

She carefully gave it to the Wiser, and than they all took seats around the table.

Graham placed it on top of the table, looking at it. It resembled a simple compass: round and black.

"Have...you asked it anything?" questioned Graham, eyeing Sue through his spectacles; his beard dangling way past the table.

The girl appeared to blush. "No...but I really did want to...but I thought it better to show it to you."

Graham smiled. It had been way too long since he had seen the compass. Professor Biggs and he was giving the compass when they were only kids.

A powerful Wiser by the name of Sheriff gave it to them as a present.

It was only to be used when needed, and they kept it around for awhile, toying with it and such. Then, their parents took it away until the children could really understand its meaning.

Afterwards, it fell into the hands of the professor when he started teaching school years later.

Now, here it was again, in Graham's reach.

"You were right, Sue. This compass is very powerful indeed. If asked the wrong question, or for fortune or gain...it will only bring bad luck."

Wriggling about his toad-stool chair like he had ants in his pants, Dingle Berry asked, "But... Uncle...the note said it could help us?"

"Yes," replied Curly Sue, "Professor Biggs said when I may need help the most. Don't you think, Graham, sir, that is what we need most now...to locate the tree!"

Graham Berry adjusted his square, black wire framed spectacles upon his button nose with laughter and a thought. How was he to tell these young ones that it was the exact opposite; that the compass did not point to a certain place (even though it was a compass) but only told general directions.

And as he recalled as a child, the directions was not that accurate. Yes, it might say to go this way or that, but you still had to find the object yourself. If asked the whereabouts of the tree it would simply state 'Go North...turn left at the rock', or something similar to the fact.

And the voice back then, years ago, was that of the old Wiser, Sheriff. Now, apparently, it was Professor Biggs' voice.

Not knowing how to go about telling them this, he would simply show them. Picking up the compass, Graham watched as the indicator spun around several times than stopped.

"Curly...Dingle...I have to show you something about this device, okay. It does help you out but not as you may think."

The young ones drew in closer to the Wiser as he tapped the black surface of the compass.

"What...is it Uncle?" questioned Dingle Berry, his young ears pointing all the way back as if a scalded pup.

Graham Berry was running out of time and days to just talk to them about it, so he might as well show them. So he held the compass to his forehead, as the two young ones watched in amazement.

"Professor Biggs...this is Graham...it has been way too long, my old friend."

The compass appeared to change shape and color; going from square to round than to black to white. Than all at once it went back to its original form.

"Hello...my old friend!" it was Professor Biggs' voice. It appeared to come directly from the compass. Curly Sue gleamed with happiness, hugging her legs with joy.

Dingle Berry almost leaped with joy from his seat, than quickly sat back down again. Graham Berry could not help as he mustered up a grin making his grey beard leap up and down.

It was true! He had not heard that voice in some time, even though he had wished that he could. His and Biggs' friendship had lasted a lifetime. Even back then as children, they would run about the forest getting into mischief.

Their parents would punish them again and again, but that did not stop their next adventures into the woods. Graham always knew it was this that got Professor Biggs into his job of searching out old houses and the such.

The Wiser slowly replied (he did not want the children to think he was happy as all get-out):

"Professor...it's been too long. Can you help us with a problem?"

Again, the compass changed with color and shape, then:

"Yes, my friend, what is it you wish to know? I'm sure Sue is there with you...and that she didn't want to question me without your assistance?"

Graham grinned again. "Yes, this is quite right."

"So...what is it you wish to know, Graham?"

At that moment the old Wiser had a million questions, but only two was worth asking. The first, of course, was of his old friend, Pilgrim: had he actually came back to life, or something else. The second question was of the Folklore Tree: if Biggs possibly knew how to begin searching for it.

As if on cue, Curly Sue butted in: "Professor Biggs...the Folklore Tree! We are in dire straits of finding its whereabouts! Can you please help us!"

From his sitting position, Graham Berry eyed her with grave concern through his glasses. It was not that he was angry with her but frustrated that she just blurted the question right out.

"Since...the question has been asked," replied Graham, "do you happen to know its whereabouts, old friend?"

The compass changed colors once more than glowed with rainbow colors this time. "The Folklore Tree...my friend? It is a hard thing to locate...but I shall try."

The old Wiser eyed the two young ones as Professor Biggs voice filled the air. It was old, but sounded exactly as it did when Biggs was alive. Sort of like a teacher who has taught for many a year.

Curly Sue grinned as Dingle Berry scudded closer to the compass Graham held.

"Yes, my old friend," replied Graham with a wide grin, making his beard dangle about.

The two young ones listened as Professor Biggs' voice echoed from the compass. It was as though he was still teaching school, but they knew this not to be true. It was but his voice, but in a way it was as if he was right in the room with them.

"The tree...my friends...exists beyond Folklore itself. First, you must travel South...than cross the waterless river."

The two young ones knew right away what Biggs was talking about. The waterless river was the same place they thought they had lost Red D. Foxx at. It was this place that they were afraid to cross, but yet again they would have to in order to locate the tree.

"Yes," replied Graham, eyeing Sue and Dingle at the same instant, "we know of this place. Than what?"

"After this...travel North, until you come across the four way path of no return. Once here, you will come across the apple trees. Travel beyond this...top the blue hill...than...and only than...will you be upon the right path."

Staring at one another, the three wondered of the words that Professor Biggs had said. They must leave very soon in search of the tree. Graham Berry knew that their time was running out...and they had to discover Bob Beaver before the weasel did.

Afterwards, they could find out the truth about what the weasel had said. If it was the truth, they would have to find the beaver, bring him here and examine the facts and try to save the kingdom.

Hours later, Graham Berry had his team picked out: it consisted of him, U.B. Einstein, Curly Sue, Dingle Berry, WC, the talking compass (with Professor Biggs' voice) and DM (the General Patton lookalike). They assembled in front of Graham's hut.

The six Smalls stood in a semi-circle awaiting their time to leave. Before this, an hour earlier,

Graham Berry had returned to his garden to the spot where Pilgrim had appeared to have left the ground.

At the fresh dirt to where his friend was laid to rest, he bent down, smoothing the soil over with his ancient hand. The compass dangled from his neck, tied to a tiny string.

Taking the compass, he slowly questioned Professor Biggs, "Professor... my old friend...what has become of Pilgrim?"

The compass glowed, shined and changed colors as if many rainbows in one. Not long after, it answered:

"Graham...my old friend...it would appear that Pilgrim has indeed returned from Na-tuate. How, I do not know, but return he has. I believe it is due to the kingdom's danger it now faces."

Slowly standing, Graham adjusted his glasses, and rubbed his long beard in deep thought.

"Than...where has he gone, Professor?"

"Beyond this place I am afraid. He has went in search of the tree as you intend to do. But, he has went in the wrong direction. You must locate him later...but first you must locate the tree. There, in only there, can you discover the truth about the weasel...the whereabouts of the beaver...and Pilgrim's location. This you must do without letting the others know. If they discover it...grave harm will befall you."

Graham Berry agreed to what the compass had said earlier. He wanted no trouble to befall them...at least not yet. But he knew somewhere down this road they must travel, dangers would surely be awaiting them.

Now, early in the morning, they all waited for the time to leave. This venture would take them, hopefully, to the Folklore Tree. And than from there, the whereabouts of the magistrate, Bob.

Graham Berry looked into Curly Sue's eyes.

"What...happened to Frank Opossum? Do you know, Sue"

"No...not really, sir. He left by the window before we got into my room. But Professor Biggs said he had to leave...for what reason he did not explain. But, he did said he would return with more details later on."

The Wiser, Graham Berry scratched his long, grey beard with thought. "Oh, ok, young one. Guess we'll know more if he returns."

"Ask the Professor," said Dingle Berry as if he had just won number one in a game of skill.

"Why not," said the Wiser, as he withdrew the compass from his pocket.

Speaking to it, he asked, "Professor, my old friend, where is the whereabouts of your friend, Frank Opossum?"

The compass turned black than white and from square to round than black again as the Professor's voice emitted from it:

"My old friend, Frank Opossum, as you know has been my cohort for some time now. And more so...after my passing. At the moment, he is waiting in the forest...where you must travel. He will locate you. But you must hurry, he has a price on his head...from the bobcat, Scarface Nelson."

At the mentioning of the name, U.B. Einstein flinched as if he had been struck by lightning.

"What is it?" questioned Graham, witnessing what his peer had done.

"I...haven't heard that name in...ages my friend."

Everyone in the group listened as Einstein recalled the memory of Scarface Nelson.

"It was many dragonfly overs ago when I was but a young Small. My parents went to visit their family...so I was all alone in my home. Little did I know that back then a member of the cat family was going to pay us a visit.

"Nelson and his family: friends of the kingdom back then...and to us all, we thought. But come to find out...when all was said and done, the Nelsons were malefactors...and they tried dealing illegal acorns and smoke within our place.

"Found out...they were made to leave...but not without a fight. Being bobcats as they were, they threatened to claw us all to bits. The Wisers back then called in the Ratz to chase the Nelsons away."

As he was talking, U.B. Einstein eyed them all one at a time, than back toward a single tree he had been gazing at for sometime that was planted neatly close to one of the inner walls.

Dingle Berry and Curly Sue were amazed at the tale that they were hearing. Never have they heard stories about crazed bobcats entering Folklore, not to mention ones that were ready for a fight.

The other Wisers' listened with amazement as well. They had heard tales of the Nelsons but not to this extent.

Einstein continued as if he had never stopped:

"The Ratz did receive our distress...and came to our rescue. But with them came a very much, younger Beelzebub. He even still had his paws back then...before they were taking off.

"It was a bloody battle indeed, my friends, but in the end the Nelson clan was chased away...vowing to return one day...to kill us all.

"That day didn't happen. Instead, Nelson the bobcat turned into a gangster living out deep within the forest...his whereabouts unknown. But, what is true, is that he had many protagonists within his group. And with that, he hires his assassins to go forth...and capture...or kill...the ones Scarface Nelson seems to dislike at the moment."

Again, his eyes darted back-and-forth among the group in front of him: Graham Berry, Curly Sue, Dingle Berry, WC, the talking compass (with Professor Biggs' voice) and DM (the General Patton lookalike).

They all returned his stare with curiosity and some fear, mostly among the young ones.

Finishing his story of Nelson the bobcat, U.B. Einstein looked to the single tree yet again. There seemed to of been some sort of breezed blowing its leaves about. With a last sentence, he replied, "They call him... Scarface Nelson now because," with an ancient finger, he ran it from his left forehead to his lower cheek, "of a scar that he had received from a fight he had got into from one of the Ratz. It was Beelzebub...if I recall correctly. A claw that left the bobcat disfigured for life!"

Dingle Berry was listening intently at the story. He had heard tales of the infamous Scarface Nelson and thought of them as such: just stories for kids. But, apparently, there was more to it than he had thought. Just think, he thought to himself, there was a gangster living within the woods of Folklore. And all of these years he never really knew that.

"And," finished Einstein for the final time, "Nelson made residence in the nearby forest. There, within his ring, he controls everything crooked about our lovely woods."

No one could believe it. Here they were about to embark on a quest to discover the Folklore Tree...than the whereabouts of Bob Beaver. But now, they all had to worry also about Scarface Nelson. Already, he had a price on Frank Opossum...and Ka-Knear only knew who was next.

Graham Berry stepped towards Einstein, patting him on the shoulder.

"Yes, my friend, I knew that you had encountered him once...but I didn't know exactly how. But, why, does it bother you so?"

U.B. Einstein slowly turned to his friend. Tears were clearly visible behind his spectacles.

"He...was the one that brought about my father's demise. Scarface Nelson...put a price on his head...I didn't know until it was too late. This is why...I shutter at that name, my friend."

No one talked after that, as they all got ready to leave the kingdom. It was almost mid-day and they had to go in search of the tree...and the beaver. So, one-after-one, they marched down the straw streets and toward the exit of the kingdom.

Smalls were standing outside their huts and stores watching as the group marched onward. Some waved goodbyes while others simply stared with wonder.

Graham Berry knew that they were thinking the same thoughts: if his group could not locate the magistrate and straighten this mess out than the kingdom would forever be lost to the Ratz.

The old Wiser wondered himself if they could actually pull this one off without a hitch. He prayed to Ka-Knear that they could.

Once outside of the kingdom, Graham Berry looked about his garden one last time. Where he had reburied the dirt upon Pilgrim's grave, a musher was now digging itself out.

The old Wiser looked to his followers as they did him. None of them knew what he had discovered, but soon, and very soon, they would. But first, they must find the tree...perhaps there...or maybe along the path...they would locate Pilgrim.

With one last glimpse, the six heroes headed outward into the unknown. Dark days were ahead and only they could, hopefully, sat it straight.

Deep within the forest beyond the kingdom was a matrix of vines and rock-laid foundations making up a massive wall of sorts. Outside of this structure was a lop-sided doorway consisting of smaller vines and thorns. Beyond this point was the lair of the sinister Scarface Nelson.

His place was well hidden from outsiders or even the Smalls if they were to pass beyond this point. From the outside, it just resembled some freak of nature hillside covered in stickers and the like.

Dimly lit with fireflies, there were tables laid all about; some had writing instruments on them while others simply contained maps of the area of the forest and beyond.

One entire section of the cave had pictures drawn with multiple animals and creatures upon them. But all had the words "captured" above them, with letters in smaller print below them which read "lol".

Scarface had proclaimed this place many dragonfly overs ago, and from here he had controlled all that was evil within the confines of the forest. Not by magical spells or acorns or even Elders' supernaturalisms, but by just the pure evil for its namesake.

He had proclaimed this place as his place of business. That was the business of selling anything and all things against the laws of the kingdom. He had a network of creatures helping him with his work. If Nelson did not like you (for any reason) he would promptly put a price on your head and have one of his henchmen hunt you down and dispose of you...so to say.

Scarface Nelson was a gangster if there ever was one, and he was proud of it. No one had dared accuse him of any misdealing...for there was never any proof or evidence pointing his way.

Now, upon his elongated, giant toadstool, he just sat back and relaxed for a moment. The bobcat had taken this place for his own after he had fought with the King Rat Beelzebub. Back then, he had almost beat the creature when the rat clawed his face from his left forehead to his lower cheek.

Barely escaping with his own life as more ratz showed up, Scarface Nelson discovered this place, making it into his domain.

Dealing with other creatures (good and bad) he had defeated them all, making them bow before him...making him top gangster among the forest dwellers.

Now with his three main thugs, he controlled everything within the forest...and than some. There were some who said his power reached beyond the forest and into nearby towns and cities. Nelson liked this...liked it a lot.

At the moment he had two things to deal with: a fox that had stolen some chickens from a ranch Nelson controlled and a opossum that went by the name Frank. The opossum was a threat just because he was helping the citizens of Folklore. This he learned from a certain acquaintanceship by the name of Salem.

Salem was a weasel whom Nelson had the misfortune of running into many years ago. They collided, only to become friends, so to say. Scarface did not trust the weasel at all, but it was the closest thing that he had to a real friend.

And for that...the gangster put a price on the opossum's head, along with another on the fox's head. The fox of course was Red D. Foxx; the one that had helped save the kingdom five years earlier.

The price was good for them both, so Nelson ordered two of his best liquidators to go and search of them: Dakota Foxx and Sierra Foxx. Both were skilled with crossbows and blades. And so far no creature they had went and search of ever escaped...or came back alive.

Chapter 4

The Compass, Location & Direction

"Yes...my bounty hunter...Dakota Foxx...I need your services but once again," replied Scarface Nelson, as he sat upon his toadstool bed. It was long and fluffy white with speckles about here and there.

In front of the gangster stood the hunter, Dakota Foxx. He was about three and a half foot tall wearing a makeshift, leather strap that held his crossbow firmly against his back. Upon his reddish head, a Robin Hood-like hat covered it, leaving the pointed ears aiming toward the heavens; also, he had on a red, skintight outfit covering up his arms and down to his ankles.

A long, reddish fluffy tail stood out from behind him as he listened to his boss.

The fox could not wait for his next mission. It had been sometime ago that he had been hired into the services of Scarface.

He did not fail then and was not going to fail this time.

"Yes, me Lord," said Dakota in an Irish accent not unlike Red D. Foxx's. "Your wish is my command." He bent down at the waist with an arm swaying outwards.

"I do not see your cohort, Sierra about," replied Nelson with a raised, hairy eyebrow.

Straighten back up, the fox explained, "Sir, she has gone out alone in search of a Wiser known as...Pilgrim. She heard that he lives again...and also searches for the Folklore Tree."

Hearing this, the gangster rubbed his grey, hairy chin then touched his scar. "Pilgrim...alive? Well...that is news indeed. Just make sure he gets dead this time!"

"Yes, sir, it shall be done. And what is the services that you require from me?"

Scarface Nelson looked to the wall that held the drawings of all that he had put a price on, than back to his bounty hunter.

"I have two new targets for you...and Sierra...when you come upon her. As far as Pilgrim...he will be a freebee."

Glancing at the stare of Dakota's face, Nelson said, "Yes, a freebee, my friend. Since I've ordered no hit on the Wiser, it will bring you nothing.

"On...the other hand...I've got a certain fox by the name of Red Damion Foxx...the price for him will be five-thousand acorns."

Nelson could tell no expression on the fox's face this time, even though his and Red had the last same names.

"Yes...he took some chickens from a friend of mine...and we wish him gone. Is that a problem, my friend?"

"No, sir, none a tall, I assure you. And the acorns...that is a good price indeed."

"I thought you might think that, Dakota. With that many acorns...you could open your own business within our kind forest. Or better yet...you could exchange them for cash of the Anti-Smalls. I know of a certain human that will trade money for acorns."

He once again eyed the hunter: his hat, crossbow and red clothes he wore. There was no expression of having known the guy or had ever heard of the guy.

"Yes, you will meet him in time...if you wish. But for now...lets get back to the business at hand."

"Yes, sir," said the bounty hunter, also eyeing his boss. Yeah, he had heard of the human that traded acorns for cash. The man was sort of weird but knew of the magic the acorns beheld.

Nelson went on: "The second trophy, you may say, is a certain opossum named Frank. He has been caught helping the Smalls at the kingdom. He must be stopped by all means.

"You did good by killing off his friend, Professor Biggs...but that just left Frank more room to run. But now...we know where he may be. Take him down, friend, and you'll get a hundred-thousand acorns...with a hundred crystals to boot!"

Dakota could not believe what he had just beheld. With that much acorns and crystals he could retire, never to hunt again...and leave the gangster once and for all.

"Sounds good, me Lord. It shall be done...as always."

At this, the bounty hunter turned, leaping from the cave and into the growing daylight outside.

Nelson waited a second, than snapped his hairy fingers of his front, left paw together. As if waiting for the signal, another fox slowly walked out from behind a hidden doorway.

It was a female fox dressed in a complete warrior outfit: the green camouflage skin-tight suit with a wrap around headband. On her waist she had a utility belt containing numerous knifes, throwing stars and other assortment of blades. On her back was strapped double, ninja swords, crisscrossed like crossbones.

Scarface Nelson grinned, his scar moving outwards.

"Follow him...Dystiny...make sure all that is is."

She bowed downward with a smile of her own.

"As always, Sire, your wish is my command."

Dystiny slowly turned and left the lair of the gangster, leaving him to his thoughts.

The sun had been out just a few hours as Graham's group turned a corner upon a forest trail. They had left the kingdom some time ago traveling in the direction the compass had told them.

Graham was leading point with the black compass still hanging on his neck by a string (still in Professor's Biggs' voice), with Dingle Berry and Curly Sue side-by-side, right behind him. After the two young ones, there were U.B. Einstein, WC and DM (the General Patton look-alike).

They were traveling South toward the waterless highway which they all knew way to well. It was there, years earlier, that they thought Red Damion

Foxx had lost his life, but only to discover later that that was not the facts.

He had survived the near-death experience, helping them to reclaim their kingdom from the evil Ratz lead by Beelzebub.

WC looked about their surroundings as they continued onward. They appeared to be walking upon a grass trail; trees and foliage dangled about everywhere it appeared; the new sun rays were just starting to pounce from one leaf to another.

The once-Wiser noticed several ladybugs dancing upon some of the large leaves as if to say hello to the pedestrians who were invading their kingdom.

Glancing more or less upwards, WC witnessed the sun as it finally revealed itself to the world above the almighty tree tops.

He smiled, knowing that all was well...at least for the time being.

"May I ask...are we heading in the right direction?"

WC had thrown the question to Graham who was still at point.

Graham Berry shook his head; his grey beard wiggling within the slight wind that had started up. The Wiser knew that the question was for him. So stopping, he turned as everyone else in the group did the same. They were all eyeing WC as if he was at some courtroom.

"Yes...my friend...we are heading in the direction in which Professor Biggs had said to go."

"Are...we sure that that...that Professor Biggs knows the whereabouts of the tree?"

Graham rubbed the black compass that dangled from his neck. "I only know...what he has told us. You know as well as I...we are heading someplace for sure. The Tree...I cannot honestly say. But at least...it is away from our kingdom."

At this, DM cleared his throat, making himself known. "As we all know...dear friends...the compass does not give pinpoint directions. It just helps you along the way. And I...for one...believe that we are headed for the Folklore Tree. If not exactly toward it...somewhere close to it."

With this, he took out a small napkin, wiping off his many medals that covered his military jacket. Why the Wiser had so many medals (they almost covered his entire jacket) was really not known by any of the others. He rarely talked about how and why he got them, only that he fought in the human/Smalls Wars of so many years ago.

And why he, and none other, received any such medals was also a mystery that he spoke little of; just that he had survived one such war, coming out alone while so many others did not.

He had told Dingle Berry once that one day he would tale his story to him; that day had never came as of yet.

Through the forest, Dystiny ran around trees, dodged overhanging limbs, and leaped a running stream. At the last second, she halted, bending to the grassy ground. Here, she picked up a small hand of soil; sniffing it.

She was on the right trek. Perhaps just a few, short minutes ago, Dakota Foxx had went this way. Looking up, she noticed a trail leading deeper into the forest terrain.

In all of her years in the service of the gangster, Bobcat Nelson, she had never liked his other two malefactor, as she referred to them. She was not jealous, but disliked them. They did not even know she existed to help Scarface, and she liked that; liked it a lot.

Standing back up, she shook herself; her green, skintight outfit wiggled with her swords and knives.

The throwing stars dangled about but never relieved themselves from her person.

Back on the trail again, she disappeared through the massive undergrowth of vines and limbs ahead. Soon, it was as if she never was.

Dakota Foxx discovered what he had been hunting for; Red Damion Foxx's scent. The lawyer of Folklore had ventured this way some time ago; perhaps looking for more chickens to devour...or something more to his liking.

Whatever the reason, Dakota had a mission to do, and do it he would. Resting next to a fallen log, he removed his crossbow slowly from behind his back.

Inspecting it, he made sure it was ready when he came across the fox. He was a bounty hunter by all means and never had he lost a chase. Dakota aimed the weapon toward a distant tree that he spotted, and slowly added an arrow to his crossbow, making ready.

The noise he heard was surely the prize the hunter was searching for.

Out from behind the tree stepped Red D. Foxx, unknowing that a bead was aimed for his head; a bead of death.

Red Damion Foxx had just left the barnyard, once again without a chicken to claim for his supper. But that would not let him down; not this time. The next time, the lawyer would make sure that Old Man Miller wasn't home, like he was before.

Yes, thought Red D. Foxx, as he stepped from behind a treeline that had a trail going deeper into the forest. Yes, next time, he would...

He heard a swooshing noise, then something striking the tree he stood beside. It just appeared there as if it had just grown out of its bark.

The fox jumped as another one struck even closer to where he was moments before. The jump appeared to had save his life. The things that struck the tree were two arrows, and they definitely were trying to strike him.

Leaping into the tall underbrush for cover, Red Foxx hide like never before. What in the Fox's

Heaven was going on? This he thought, looking about the tree lines and distant forest scenes.

Someone was out to get him and it sure was not Old Man Miller and his shotgun.

Across the pasture of sorts, the lawyer saw who it was: another fox dressed in some sort of red, skin-tight outfit, wearing a green hat. And he was welding some sort of weapon the likes of which Red Foxx had never seen before, or had he.

Yes, it was a crossbow like the ratz had used years ago while trying to take over the kingdom, but in much larger scale. And, another arrow had already been added to it, aiming his way.

Of all of his years, Foxx had never ran across anything like this. Why was someone out to get him?

Had he did something wrong to upset that crazy fox?

With this thought, Red D. Foxx had a plan. Well, not exactly a plan of sorts, but it may add to why this creature was after him, and give him the time to escape...hopefully.

So, the lawyer cleared his throat, peered around one last time, and simply asked:

"Or you CRAZY? What are you trying to do: kill me?"

The hit-fox was close to a hollow in an old tree trunk; a tree trunk that Red Damion Foxx knew all too well. It was his home; where he had received the Snail-mail massages about the Smalls' trial so long ago.

But, wondered the lawyer fox, how did that other fox know where he lived? Or for that matter, how did he know where to find his home?

Maybe, the red fox plundered on, the hit-fox fox did not know about it at all. Maybe, he was there by pure coincidence.

Dakota Foxx held his crossbow steady; aiming for the distant target he had discovered. Looking across the green pasture at the other fox's snout, he simply replied to the question:

"As a matter of fact...yes I am...Red Damion Foxx! My head honcho has put a price on your head, my friend. And I never lose one of those. So, if you'll simply step out so I can see you...I'll make it quick; you won't feel a thing, I assure you!"

Red D. Foxx did not like the sound of that; no, not at all. And he sure as hell was not about to step out giving that other fox a clear shot. So, what was he going do? This thought ate at Foxx's brain; so much in fact that he was trying to figure a way out of this trap.

What would he do if he was one of Old Man Miller's chickens? This thought ate at his thoughts just as he heard a limb snap from the opposite direction of the hit-fox. Spinning around, he could not believe what he witnessed: another fox was perhaps thirty yards away, next to some trees. It was a female wearing a green-tight outfit that almost made her blend in with her surroundings.

Two ninja swords were strapped, crisscrossed to her back, and around her waist were numerous knifes and things that resembled tiny, pointed stars. Red Foxx knew instantly that they were weapons, and could easily fly his direction.

But, all-and-all, the fox did not notice the arrow weapon that she must of shot toward him moments before.

Than he quickly saw it; another fox (a third one) came from the left, perhaps fifty yards from the female fox. This one was another female; baring a crossbow as the first fox that had tried to kill him.

Red Damion Foxx could not believe what he was seeing. In all of his years, never has someone tried to take him out in this sort of way; especially three hit-foxes.

With disbelief in his old eyes, the fox dodged behind the bushes where he stood. How in all that was good was he going to get out of this mess?

Some miles from the kingdom, Graham Berry once more questioned the compass that dangled from his neck. They had traveled into the forest just south of Folklore as Professor Bigg's voice had said to do. Somewhere up ahead existed the waterless highway that had taken Red Damion Foxx's life so many years ago.

"Are we on the right trek, my old friend?"

The compass changed shape and color once more, than answered:

"Yes, old friend, take this direction until the river of no water is approached. Than from there, cross it and travel through the underbrush. Afterwards, I shall tell you more."

The group listened as this was said, Graham in front, with the others just behind. WC followed the Wiser; behind him walked U.B. Einstein, Curly Sue and Dingle Berry. Not far behind the group was DM, the General Patton lookalike of the human wars so long ago.

As he stepped across a fallen branch, the compass swung this way and that, seeming in danger of breaking from the string that held it. Holding it by its metal casing, Graham Berry was not about to lose it, hopefully.

U.B. Einstein stepped up to his old friend, Graham, and looked about the forest they were traveling. Massive pine trees loomed above them like some weird oddity of a cave. As small as they were, any tree, even a tiny bush, could easily engulf them as if they were not even there.

"My friend," Einstein questioned, "or we sure we are doing the right thing? I mean...could we simply go back and not let that weasel have the kingdom. I mean...after all, we could fight 'em off."

Graham grinned at his old friend. "Yes, we could do that, but remember if what he said is true...even the kingdom would abide by what has happened. Nature...itself would throw us out, my friend. You know this to be true. I like it no more than you...but we must find another way; another way to keep our home."

"But...how?"

Graham Berry looked about the path they were walking.

"I believe...the Folklore Tree is our only chance...and the magistrate, Bob Beaver is the law of Folklore; its magic and power. What he says could...and will...change everything."

U.B. Einstein stepped over a small, moving ladybug as it crossed the leafy path. The tiny insect stopped, looking up at the strangers that had evaded its territory.

"Hey...friends," the ladybug said in a very tiny girl's voice, "where forth are y'all headed?" The miniature voice was very low, but in a German accent.

The group of travelers came to a halt as the ladybug talked.

This did not amaze them at all, but rather intrigued them.

In a whisper, Einstein asked Graham, "But what if...he says we...are in the wrong, and must leave?"

"Than...we leave...my friend."

They talked quietly not wanting others to hear, as the ladybug once again asked the same question.

The group circled the tiny, black and red-dotted insect.

Graham touched the dangling compass with wonder. Perhaps they could ask the ladybug the way to the tree; it may know something or two.

"Hi...little friend...and what are you called...may I ask?"

The insect flapped its tiny miniature wings, circled a bit, than looked up to what she considered to be giants.

"Why...I am called Diane, my friends. And...whom may you be?"

Graham introduced himself and his group, than asked Diane the question that was on everyone's mind at the moment:

"We were wondering...do you know the whereabouts of...the Folklore Tree? That is where we are headed."

The ladybug, Diane, smiled at her new friends, than simply answered:

"I do...not really know where it is, but I have heard of it. You are on the right track...I know that for sure."

The group all looked to one another with smiles; at least they were headed right. Than from out of the blue, WC asked:

"If you don't know where it is...than how can you possibly know we are heading right?"

Diane the ladybug circled again, flapped her wings, and stared at the Wiser.

"'cause...my giant friend...many have taken this path...and many have said they seen the tree."

This seemed to satisfy the group, as Graham Berry leaned down, softly patting the insect. The ladybug's miniature wings flapped once more, than Diane took to the heavens, disappearing into the distant foliage of plant life.

"Did...that answer your question?" asked Graham to WC. "Are you satisfied?"

The once Wiser grinned. "Yes...my friend, I suppose I am."

The group once more continued toward the distant, waterless highway that would in turn, hopefully, take them to the Folklore Tree.

Red Damion Foxx could take it no longer, so he dashed from behind his cover of bushes. With a quick glance behind, he noticed the three hit-foxes in hot pursuit; weapons aimed, armed and ready.

Leaping a nearby, fallen log Foxx tripped on some sharp vines that appeared to come from nowhere. Falling, he tried to regain his balance, but it was way too late. His legs were tangled as if the vines were helping the crazed foxes that wanted his head.

The once lawyer fox could hear the approaching sounds of the hunters as they came nearer. Trying like crazy, he could not get the sharp vines from his legs as an arrow flew, sticking into the side of a nearby tree.

With another look toward his adversaries, he saw that they were all to close for comfort. If they got to him now, Red Damion Foxx was a goner for sure.

With a snap of a distant branch, he knew that his days were numbered; perhaps this would be his last moment on earth.

Now Red Damion Foxx knew how all of the chickens he had snatched up in the past must have felt; they knew their time was up, just as surely as he knew his time was up.

Before Red Foxx could take a second breath, the three hunters had surrounded him. Like a rabbit in a snare, he was done for.

Dakota Foxx aimed his crossbow straight for his prey's head, and with a wide grin said, "Pray to your god...Red...this is your last moment on earth. There shall be no other day for you!"

Red Foxx closed his eyes, waiting for the arrow to seize his forehead like some mighty hammer.

Than the last thing the lawyer heard was the click of the bow.

To be Continued with

Part 2:

The Weasel

(Coming Soon)

SNEAK PEEK

Graham's group enters a dark forest that appears to be alive with anything but plant life. Within this place, they discover the Folklore Tree that was thought to be just a myth; a legend.

From here, they learn of the whereabouts of Bob the Beaver, the only one that may be able to save their kingdom.

But all is not as what it seems; getting to the magistrate is more difficult than first imagined. He lives beneath a lighthouse within a massive maze of underground tunnels. One wrong move, it could mean the end for our heroes.

Meal while, the weasel called Salem, discovers his old friend, Scarface Nelson, the gangster. He tells of Foxx's demise at the hands of his hunters. If ever a weasel could smile, this one did.

Next, they would take the kingdom, using its magic and power to destroy all of the remaining Smalls...and than the human race as well.

Yes, it was a good day to be a gangster...and Scarface knew it to be so.

7871856R00099

Printed in Great Britain
by Amazon.co.uk, Ltd.,
Marston Gate.